Soccer Song

Green Light Readers
Harcourt, Inc.
Orlando   Austin   New York
San Diego   London

Meow

Soccer Song

Patricia Reilly Giff

Illustrated by **Blanche Sims**

Jill had long arms.
She had strong hands.

One day, Jill got Gus.
"Jill did it!" called Tom.
"Meow," said Gus.

One day, Fran swung the bat.
Her ball went up.
Jill jumped up.

"Jill got it!" yelled the kids.
"Meow," said Gus.

At school, Miss King said,
"It's soccer time! Kick the ball
with your feet."

"Don't use your hands!" said Tom.

Jill's legs went this way.
The ball went that way.

Jill's head went this way.
The ball went that way.

Jill hung her head.

"You have strong arms and hands,"
said Tom. "You got Gus out of a tree."
"You got my ball, too," said Fran.

"A goalie can use her hands,"
said Miss King.

The next day, Jill was goalie.
She used her strong arms and hands.
She blocked the ball every time.

"You did it!" yelled Tom and Fran.
"Jump, block! I am strong!
This is my soccer song!" sang Jill.
"Meow!" sang Gus.

What Do You Think?

Does Jill have trouble learning to play soccer at first? If so, why?

What are some things that Jill can do well? Make a list.

Why is Jill a good goalie?

Do you think Jill will keep playing soccer? Why or why not?

Write about something you do well.

Meet the Author
Patricia Reilly Giff

Patricia Reilly Giff has written many books. In her stories, children do some of the same things you do! "I enjoyed writing this story because my grandchildren love soccer. My granddaughter's name is Jillian. We call her Jill, just like the character in my story."

Meet the Illustrator
Blanche Sims

Blanche Sims has illustrated many children's books. She says that the best part about being an artist is drawing. She has always loved to draw! When Blanche Sims was in school, one of her teachers even hung up a huge piece of paper in the classroom for her to fill with her artwork.

Meow

For information about permission to reproduce selections from this book, please write to Permissions, Houghton Mifflin Harcourt Publishing Company 215 Park Avenue South NY NY 10003.

www.hmhco.com

First Green Light Readers edition 2008

Green Light Readers and its logo are trademarks of Houghton Mifflin Harcourt Publishing Company, registered in the United States of America and/or other jurisdictions.

Library of Congress Cataloging-in-Publication Data
Giff, Patricia Reilly.
Soccer song/Patricia Reilly Giff; illustrated by Blanche Sims.
p. cm.
"Green Light Readers."
Summary: Jill's friends know that she has strong arms and hands and so when she is learning to play soccer, they help her to find a position in which she can excel.
[1. Soccer—Fiction. 2. Ability—Fiction. 3. Individuality—Fiction.] I. Sims, Blanche, ill.
II. Title.
PZ7.G3626Soc 2008
[E]—dc22   2007042342
ISBN 978-0-15-206571-3
ISBN 978-0-15-206565-2 (pb)

SCP 8 7 6
4500512255

Ages 5–7
Grade: 1
Guided Reading Level: D
Reading Recovery Level: 6

Green Light Readers
For the reader who's ready to GO!

"A must-have for any family with a beginning reader."—*Boston Sunday Herald*

"You can't go wrong with adding several copies of these terrific books to your beginning-to-read collection."—*School Library Journal*

"A winner for the beginner."—*Booklist*

Five Tips to Help Your Child Become a Great Reader

1. Get involved. Reading aloud to and with your child is just as important as encouraging your child to read independently.

2. Be curious. Ask questions about what your child is reading.

3. Make reading fun. Allow your child to pick books on subjects that interest her or him.

4. Words are everywhere—not just in books. Practice reading signs, packages, and cereal boxes with your child.

5. Set a good example. Make sure your child sees YOU reading.

Why Green Light Readers Is the Best Series for Your New Reader

• Created exclusively for beginning readers by some of the biggest and brightest names in children's books

• Reinforces the reading skills your child is learning in school

• Encourages children to read—and finish—books by themselves

• Offers extra enrichment through fun, age-appropriate activities unique to each story

• Incorporates characteristics of the Reading Recovery program used by educators

• Developed with Harcourt School Publishers and credentialed educational consultants